The Fox and the Abandoned Puppies

Jackie L. Mustoe

MINERVA PRESS
LONDON
ATLANTA MONTREUX SYDNEY

ISBN 0 75410 316 1

First Published 1998 by
MINERVA PRESS
315–317 Regent Street
London W1R 7YB

2nd Impression 1999

Printed in Great Britain for Minerva Press

The Fox and the Abandoned Puppies

Acknowledgements

I would like to thank my very dear husband, Allan Michael Mustoe, for his knowledge of nature and wonderful craft of storytelling. Without him, this book would not have been possible.

Contents

Chapter One

The Night it Snowed

Sophie May was a little girl who was six years old, had beautiful long, blonde curly hair, big blue eyes with long dark eyelashes, rosy cheeks and the cutest, little rosebud mouth.

She lived far into the beautiful countryside of the Cotswolds with her mother and father, Audrey and Sam, in a quaint, chocolate-box Cotswold cottage, which was situated right by the side of a wood where Sophie spent a lot of her time playing and where her father had made her a den.

As Sophie was such a kind little girl, all the animals in the wood were very fond of her and kept a watchful eye over her when she was out playing.

She did not have any brothers or sisters and, because she lived so far out in the countryside, she sometimes became a little lonely.

One January morning, she woke up early. She knelt up on her bed and peered through the curtains. It was still very dark but there was something different out there that she could not quite make out. She looked harder, and as her eyes became used to the dark, she could see what it was.

It's been snowing, she said to herself, then she quickly scrambled off her bed and ran into her parent's bedroom.

'It's been snowing, it's been snowing,' Sophie shouted, shaking her mother's shoulder.

Her mother groaned; she had been having such a lovely dream. She rolled over and switched on her bedside lamp, and looked at the clock.

'Oh Sophie, it's only half past five, why are you awake this early, you little monkey?'

'Oh, Mummy, it's been snowing, I'll be able to build a snowman and…'

'Hold on a minute, Sophie,' said her mother cutting in. 'Stop getting so excited, it'll still be there when we get up at a more respectable time. You can't do anything while it's still dark. Your dad will be getting up soon for work so we will all get up then, have some breakfast and go out and play. Meanwhile, hop in here and go to sleep.'

'Well, if there's been a lot of snow, I won't be going to work today,' said her father, rolling over to face Sophie, as she climbed in over her mother and squeezed between them with a cheeky smile.

'Oh, goody, you can help me build a snowman then.'

Sophie's mother switched off the light and they all snuggled down and fell back off to sleep.

Sophie woke to find that both her parents had got up and left her to sleep on. She climbed out of bed and ran to the window. She couldn't believe her eyes. Everywhere was completely white, as if a fairy had come in the middle of the night and draped a white blanket over everything. She squealed with delight and ran to her bedroom and quickly got dressed. She nipped into the bathroom on her way down and just rubbed a flannel over her face and cleaned her teeth. She could smell bacon being cooked in the kitchen. Sophie loved their kitchen. It was a large room, a traditional old farmhouse kitchen. It had pine cupboards at one end, by the side of these was a deep, rectangular white china sink with wooden draining boards on either side. This was situated in front of the window which looked out on to the vegetable and herb garden. At the other end was a large pine kitchen table, this too was rectangular with six high-backed pine kitchen chairs placed around it, but Sophie's favourite thing in the kitchen was the Rayburn. This was a large square, cast-iron cooker, but unlike modern cookers, it did not run on gas or electricity. On the front of the cooker, on the right-hand side, was a large square glass door and inside was a large oven where Sophie's mum baked scrumptious cakes and biscuits. Below this was a drawer which was a plate warmer, but on the left-hand side there was another door which opened into a fireplace where you burnt wood and coal, collectively known as solid fuel. This fire made the whole cooker hot. As well as cooking, it dried wet clothes beautifully when they were hung in front of it, it also had a back boiler which enabled it to heat all their hot water. It was indispensable. The kitchen was always warm and welcoming and it always seemed to smell of delicious cooking.

She ran downstairs into the kitchen; her mother turned and gave her a warm smile.

12

'Well, you took your time in getting up, considering you were the one that was up at the crack of dawn.'

Her father ruffled her curls affectionately as she sat down beside him at the kitchen table and reached for the box of cornflakes.

'Are you going to work today, Daddy?'

'Not today, or for a few days, looking at how much snow we had in the night.'

'Oh goody, we'll be able to start the snowman.' said Sophie getting up from the table, her cornflakes half eaten.

'Only when you have finished your breakfast; and don't eat it too fast or you'll end up getting indigestion.'

Sophie sat back down to finish her cereal. Her mother walked over to the table carrying two plates of bacon and eggs which were for herself and Sam.

'Cor, that's just what the doctor ordered,' said Sam, his mouth watering at the look and smell of the appetising breakfast. Audrey was a wonderful cook.

'Well, tuck in, there's plenty. Would you like some when you've finished your cornflakes, Sophie?'

Sophie looked up and shook her head. The cereal was more than enough.

'Didn't that wind blow last night? It woke me up in the early hours; it sounded just like an aeroplane's engine revving up.'

'Well, I didn't hear a thing, I slept like a log,' replied Sam, in-between a mouthful of bacon and egg.

Audrey looked at the pair of them. 'No, you two certainly do sleep well, you never hear a thing either of you.'

Sophie and her father looked at each other and smiled. Once their heads touched their pillows, they were off in their own little dream worlds.

Sophie finished her cornflakes and slid down off the kitchen chair. 'May I go outside and play now, Mummy?'

'Yes, but you must wrap up warm. Put your scarf and that woollen pompon hat on, which I bought you the other day, that will keep your ears nice and warm, and put on another jumper and your red new anorak that Grandma bought you for Christmas.'

Sophie ran upstairs to her bedroom and found all her things neat and tidy in her wardrobe. Her red anorak was hung on a coat hanger and her scarf and hat were on the shelf. But where were her gloves? She had had them on yesterday. She looked through her other clothes in her wardrobe and then through her drawers but she still couldn't find them.

'Mummy, I can't find my gloves.' Sophie shouted, as she ran down the stairs and into the kitchen.

'They're here by the Rayburn. I put them there last night as you got them wet yesterday, and here are your wellingtons.'

Her wellington boots were red, to match her anorak, whilst her gloves, scarf and hat were blue. She looked lovely with all her blonde curls peeping out from underneath her hat. Sophie was now ready.

'I'll be out shortly to help you with your snowman, Sophie, and try not to get too wet,' said her father, who was now tucking into his second helping of bacon and eggs.

Sophie turned and beamed at her mother and father, then out she went. She breathed in sharply, it was very cold and very still. The wind had gone completely. As she walked, she made little imprints in the snow. She began to walk a little faster, then faster still, until she was running in a small circle, then splodge. Sophie fell flat on her face. She pushed herself up and giggled. Her warm breath against the frosty cold air was like steam from a train puffing along a railway track.

'That was fun, I fell over but I didn't hurt myself,' so she hurled herself into the snow again and again until she was quite exhausted. By this time she was extremely wet but as she was having such good fun she hadn't noticed.

The kitchen door opened and out came her father. 'Ready to make your snowman now, Sophie?'

'Oh yes, please.'

Sophie went running over to him, her clothes and hair wet through, her cheeks glowing with the cold and excitement.

'Oh, Sophie, I told you not to get too wet, you're soaking, you'll have to go in now and change.'

'Oh no, Daddy, I'm not cold, really I'm not.' Sophie was desperate not to have to go back in, it would take for ever to change all of her clothes. Her father opened the kitchen door and ushered her inside.

'Look at this, Audrey, Sophie is wet through.'

Her mother came over and smiled. She remembered when she used to do the same when she was a little girl. She took off Sophie's wellingtons and anorak and took her upstairs to put some dry clothes

on her. It didn't take that long, much to Sophie's relief, and soon she was outside again. She and her father began to build the snowman, he had some old clothes in the garden shed and also an old pipe which he used to smoke at one time.

He got it down off the shelf and smiled to himself, 'I knew this would come in handy one day.'

Sophie, meanwhile, was getting some coal from the coal bunker to make the snowman's eyes and buttons for his coat. Then, ran to the kitchen and asked her mother if she had either a spare carrot or parsnip which she could use as the nose. The snowman was starting to take shape rather nicely.

Sophie's mother came out with some mugs of steaming hot chocolate. She too had dressed in her outside clothes and was going to help finish off the snowman.

The sun was just starting to get a little warmer. It was a lovely, fresh, crisp day. The sky was a clear, pale blue colour. In the far off distance you could hear some dogs barking. There were some rabbits out in the field looking for something to eat, but it was all under the snow.

'I'll bring some cabbage leaves out for those rabbits, they won't find anything to eat now for days with all this snow about.'

'It makes you wonder, Audrey, how anything copes in this weather. If anything got caught out in it last night they would be in a desperate state this morning.'

Sophie looked up at her father with a sad little face. She hated to think of animals being in distress of any kind. She hoped with all her heart that all the animals had been down in their little burrows far away from the howling wind and swirling snow.

Sophie shivered which her mother noticed.

'Come on, Sophie, let's get you inside and by that fire, you're starting to get cold.'

She smiled and nodded to her mother. She was getting rather cold but she knew she would soon be nice and warm by the lovely old Rayburn.

'But we haven't finished the snowman, Mummy.'

'Don't you worry about that, the snow will still be here later when you come back out, you can finish him off then.'

Sophie and her mother walked back across the lawn to the kitchen door, took off their boots and in they both went.

Sam looked up at the sky. The clouds were starting to gather and it was getting decidedly colder. 'We're going to have a lot more snow yet, it's a good job we've got all our coal and wood in.'

He looked at the half finished snowman, then picked up the clothes, the carrot, the pipe and the bits of coal which Sophie had brought over and took them back to the garden shed. It started to snow, Sam turned up his collar.

'Sophie won't be coming out here again today, the weather is going to get much worse. I'd better make sure that everything is safe and secure.'

He locked up the garden shed, then walked over to the bird table and made sure that there was plenty of food on it, had one last walk round the garden then made his way back to the warm comfort of the kitchen.

'Before you come in, Sam, quickly nip these cabbage leaves over in to the field.'

Audrey handed him a bagful. She was always careful not to throw anything away that she knew the woodland animals would be able to eat. Sometimes, when she didn't have enough leftovers she would use a perfectly good cabbage from her pantry and give to the rabbits. Sam and Audrey had always been ardent animal lovers right from when they were children.

They had met at the local Young Farmers Club, found that they had a lot in common, not just their love for animals but for books, films and the theatre. They married a year after they had met and now lived right out in the middle of nowhere by the side of a wood. It was an animal lovers paradise and they were now teaching Sophie everything they knew and were so pleased that she loved animals just as much as they did.

They always made sure that all the woodland animals had plenty to eat in winter. They bought special nuts for the blue tits which they put into little wire tubes that hung all around the garden; barley and oats which they scattered round the lawn for the larger birds; and any leftovers such as bacon rind, bread and biscuits were put on the bird table. They bought dog biscuits for the foxes and a little hay for the odd roving deer which Sophie was always so pleased to see.

Sam went back to the house when he had finished putting out the cabbage leaves. He took off his Wellington boots and put them on some newspaper by the Rayburn then hung up his coat. Sophie was sitting up at the kitchen table, drinking another cup of hot chocolate, her legs swinging underneath the table as they weren't yet quite long enough to touch the floor.

'Well, Sophie, we won't be going out again today, it looks like the weather has set in for a bit, but that won't bother us, eh, Sophie?' tweaking her little nose as he walked by.

She finished her hot chocolate and wandered over to the kitchen door. It had glass panes right to the floor so she could look through it. She could only just make out her half finished snowman as it was now snowing very heavily. The wind was also starting to howl ferociously and Sophie hoped that all the animals were all safe and sound in their homes, just like she was.

For the rest of the day Sophie and her parents sat in their lounge doing puzzles, jigsaws and some drawing. Soon it was time for tea and then Sophie's bath then bedtime. She said 'Night night' to her father before giving him a big kiss and a cuddle, then her mother took her upstairs to bed.

They both looked through the bedroom window, it was very dark but they could still see the snow falling thickly and hear the wind howling through the trees. The Cotswold stone wall at the front of the house had completely disappeared under a blanket of snow. Sophie was fascinated, she had never seen snow like this before. She couldn't wait for morning when she would be able to finish off her snowman, and perhaps her father would make her a sledge and take her sledging down in the valley.

'Come on, then Sophie, let's get you tucked up in your little bed, "As snug as a bug in a rug", as my mother used to say. Now, what story would you like

tonight? What about *The Snowman* that you had for Christmas?'

Sophie nodded and snuggled up to her teddy. Her mother began telling her the story about the snowman and the little boy flying through the air. Sophie was soon fast asleep and dreaming of the snowman, but instead of the little boy on the snowman's back, it was herself, high above the clouds flying with the snowman.

Sophie's mother and father went to bed at about half past nine. They were never very late as they were such early risers.

'I reckon we'll be snowed in for at least a week,' said Sam pulling up the thick woollen blankets over Audrey and himself.

'Oh well, it doesn't bother us, we've got plenty to eat and plenty of firewood, so we won't go without. I think it's quite exciting being marooned on our own little island, so to speak, don't you, Sam?'

'Aye, that I do.' He switched off the bedside lamp and they both snuggled down in the nice warm bed, knowing that they were all warm and safe from the wicked weather.

Chapter Two

The Wood at Night

Outside, the weather was getting extremely bad. The snow was falling so thick and fast you couldn't see a yard in front of you. There was nothing left untouched by the icy hands of Jack Frost. It was getting deeper by the minute. Sophie's father had been right, they would not be able to move for at least a week, if not longer. All the roads were now impassable except for a very few main roads which had to be kept open for the emergency services, but even these were getting more difficult to keep clear. The snowploughs were working flat out.

All the rabbits were down in their burrows snuggled up together fast asleep, except for Mr Ronald Rabbit, who was getting rather concerned because he knew that he had to keep their entrance to their burrow clear or they would suffocate or starve to death. He knew that when they were able to move, the kind people who lived in the cottage by the side of the wood would leave some food out for them. They normally did when the weather was bad but it had not been this bad for several years.

He lit the lamp next to his chair and made his way up the passage to their front door. He hung up the

lamp, unbolted the door and cautiously opened it. The wind blew hard and a flurry of snow came swirling through the door. Mr Ronald Rabbit quickly closed it and was relieved to see that his lamp was still alight. He took it down off the hook and went back down the passage.

Mrs Rosie Rabbit was now up out of her chair and looking concerned, 'you haven't been outside, have you Ronald?'

'No, Rosie, dear. I just went up to see if our doorway was blocked but I had to shut the door quickly or we would have had a load of snow in our hallway, so I couldn't see much at all. We will just have to wait until morning, but there now, don't you start worrying,' said Ronald, putting his arm around his frightened wife. 'If it is blocked, the other animals and birds, like Mr and Mrs Brocklehurst the Badgers, Douglas Deer and Freddie Pheasant, will come looking for us and dig us out. Now let's get to bed as I think we've got quite a busy day ahead of us.'

The weather was now beginning to do a lot of damage to the wood and surrounding countryside. Trees were carrying heavy amounts of snow upon their boughs. Some of the older trees were finding it too much of a strain to bear the weight any longer. Their old, twisted boughs snapped like matchsticks; the wind being so strong it was uprooting trees in its path, and so loud it was deafening. Indeed, the weather was certainly taking its toll.

All the animals in the wood were trying to sleep through this loud snowstorm but it wasn't that easy. A pair of pheasants had been woken with a start as the branch which they had been roosting on had snapped from underneath them, luckily they had been thrown clear and so only their pride was hurt. They dusted themselves down quickly and flew into the next tree, gripping hard with their claws so as not to get blown away. They put their heads into their chests and tried to get to sleep again. The stoats and weasels were all curled up in their little houses, but the luckiest of all the animals were the hedgehogs, who had hibernated earlier on in the year and so didn't know what was going on outside their nests. The owls had flown back to their cosy homes still hungry as the weather was far too bad for them to be out hunting and they knew that they wouldn't find anything to eat. It was best for them to save their energy and keep as warm as they could and try again in the morning.

The deer were all huddled up together underneath the large oak tree, which had become their home the same winter that Sam and Audrey had moved in to their cottage. They had seen them from afar and they gradually realised that they loved animals and that no harm would come to them as long as they stayed near the little cottage.

The only animal that was out in this awful weather was Mrs Fox.

Chapter Three

The Brave Cotswold Fox

Mrs Fox had been visiting her old and dear friend over at Sheepriver Wood. Her friend always made her extremely welcome and they would while away the time reminiscing, and have a thoroughly good time.

Today, however, with the weather starting to turn for the worst, Mrs Fox and her friend, Mrs Brush were unusually very hungry so they had decided to go and visit the local farmer and see if there were any loose hens about so they could have roast chicken for their lunch.

They had made their way down to Mistletoe Farm and, to their delight, had spied a lovely big fat hen which would satisfy them both. Unfortunately, the hen had made such a lot of noise, the farmer had come out to see what all the commotion was about and he saw the two foxes run off with his most prized hen. Mrs Fox and Mrs Brush ran like the wind with their spoils, back to the den deep in the wood where nobody would find them. They had an enormous feast and while they ate with gluttony, they laughed till the tears rolled down their cheeks about how they had outran the farmer and the expression on his face when he had seen them with his hen.

It was now three o'clock and Mrs Fox made her move to leave. She thanked her friend for the lively antics of the morning and her hospitality, kissed her affectionately on both cheeks and bid her farewell.

She was pleased she had left early as she knew the atrocious weather was coming soon. All she wanted to do now was get home as fast as she could where she would be safe and warm. It was quite a few miles back to her house which was in the wood by the side of Sam and Audrey's cottage, which was known as Hawkes Clump. It was a real haven for animals and birds alike, as they had bought it off Colonel Gepsy along with their cottage some years ago and they had then put a complete ban on the wood ever being hunted or shot again.

As she approached Sheep Bridge Bottom, she sensed all was not well. She looked up the valley which was home to the local flock of sheep. It was common-place to see the flock spread out all over the valley, but this afternoon, they were all huddled together up against the Cotswold stone wall which was shelter from the bitter East wind. She approached cautiously, the sheep knew Mrs Fox very well but she didn't want to make them jump and run away as this would draw attention to them all. She made her way amongst them and eventually found her old ewe friend Trip, so called as she always produced and raised at lambing time the most lovable and charming set of triplets you could ever wish to see.

'What on earth are you doing out this time of day, I would have thought you would be tucked up in your

den? The weather's on the turn you know, heavy snowfalls are due this evening.'

'I'm just making my way home, I've been over to see Mrs Brush, you know, my friend who lives in Sheepriver Wood.'

'I hope you two weren't the ones responsible for taking off the prize hen that belongs to Colonel Gepsy. He is not pleased, not pleased at all.'

'Well, actually, we did get a bit hungry and we did have a wander down to Mistletoe Farm and we did see a big fat hen which was there for the taking.'

Trip looked at her disapprovingly, 'Well, you've got yourself a stack of trouble this time. I overheard the gamekeeper telling Luke, the shepherd, that they are out to get you, they said enough is enough.'

'Who, exactly, is out to get me?' asked Mrs Fox, starting to feel the hair on the back of her neck rising.

'There's Colonel Gepsy and his two Alsatians…

'Oh, they're all right, I can outwit those two.'

But Trip had not finished. Mrs Fox looked at Trip with concern.

'Who else?'

'Jebb.'

'No,' replied Mrs Fox.

She was worried now. Jebb was the estate's game-keeper. His job was to breed as many pheasants as he could for the winter sport of the gentry, pheasant shooting, and any animal or bird that interfered with this had to be dealt with severely. Rabbits and hares, who would inevitably graze on the young sweet spring grasses and sometimes indulge on a few new shoots of the farmer's cereal crops, would also face the wrath of

Jebb's twelve-bore shotgun. Whenever he was out and about on the estate, it was run, hide, climb, burrow, jump, fly, anything to keep out of the sight of this heartless, brutal and vicious man. The best form of defence was the buzzards who soared high up into the sky and would let out a high pitched screech to warn them that the killing machine was on the move. Mrs Fox had seen him many a morning from a safe distance loading up the Land Rover with his kill. She too had had many a run-in with him and his two black Labradors, but always just managed to get away by the skin of her teeth. Maybe this was the last time. She had to think fast and muster all of her cunning.

'You will have to leave now, the shepherd will be along soon doing his early evening round and he's had his instructions directly from the Colonel to keep his eye out for you and report back.'

Luke, the shepherd, didn't mind Mrs Fox as she never did his sheep or his lambs any harm. He thought it a mighty fine sight to see a wily old fox crossing the valley. He remembered once with much sadness the time when he had been a young shepherd trying to make a reputation for himself. He had seen a fox near to his field of ewes with young lambs and he had raised his twelve bore shotgun and fired it towards the fox. The scream that came from that injured animal had never left him. He ran straight over to where the maimed animal lay. Her beautiful brown eyes had looked at him with such sadness that this tough young man broke down and cried. He remembered lifting the fox into his link box on the back of his tractor with such tenderness. How could a human being inflict such pain on to such a beautiful animal. He had vowed there and then that he would never raise his gun again. He had taken the fox home, carefully extracted the shot from her leg, and nursed her back to full health over the next few weeks. Then he'd released her back into the wild and he would sometimes catch a glimpse of her early in the morning making her way back to her den after a night's hunting.

In the distance you could see the lights of Luke's tractor coming across the valley and hear the sound of the old diesel engine.

'On your way, old friend, and take care, you only have a certain amount of chances you know. They are waiting for you in the Land Rover down at the bottom of the hollow and they have got those lights, you know, the ones they use for rabbiting. As soon as you raided Mistletoe Farm, they loaded them up into the back of the vehicle, drove down to the hollow and have been there ever since.'

'How did they know where to wait? Am I getting so predictable?'

'I think they worked out it was you and knew you had to get back to your den in Hawkes Clump and that you wouldn't be able to go over the top with the deep snow. They knew the hollow was your only route. They'll wait all night if they have to. Go now, go,' urged Trip, 'The Shepherd is nearly here.'

The sheep started to bleat and stamp their feet nervously as Mrs Fox climbed over the wall. They knew something was amiss.

'What's all the noise about?' shouted Luke, as he climbed down out of his tractor, its lights shining into the flock of sheep, picking out the snow, glistening where it was stuck and hanging down off their long woolly coats. 'Is that old fox in there with you?'

Even if it was, he wasn't going to say a thing, he only wished it well. He thought it quite amusing taking the Colonel's prize hen.

The snow began to fall, the weather was beginning to turn. Mrs Fox was very frightened. Her eyes were darting this way and that, peering through the large flakes which were now falling steadily, her ears springing backwards and forwards as she strained to hear anything which would give her a clue regarding her safety.

Have I overdone it this time? Mrs Fox asked herself, her heart thudding in her small chest.

She arrived at the old burnt-out elm stumps on the brow of the valley, looking down to the hollow, keeping well out of sight. She had to cross over the farm track which ran through the valley. She would be safe if she got to the other side. Over there was a small plantation of ash trees which were overgrown with blackthorn, the foxes' favourite tree. No man or animal would ever get the better of a fox in blackthorn, but first, she had to get there.

The wind was now getting up and the snow falling even more thickly. It would give her a bit of cover, but not enough to quell the enthusiasm of Jebb. He was standing by the side of the Land Rover with his dogs, his gun poised ready, his eyes peering into the gloom, his cap and the shoulders of his waxed jacket were getting covered in snow, but it didn't bother Jebb. He was hungry for her, he had been after her for years but she had always managed to get back to Hawkes Clump where he was not able to touch her. He rued the day when Colonel Gepsy had sold Hawkes Clump to Sam and Audrey. All the animals that lived on the estate seemed to be making their homes there. He hadn't been able to fill his gamebags in a long time.

Colonel Gepsy stood on the other side of the vehicle with his two Alsatians. He and his two dogs were getting rather cheesed off with the waiting and they were getting cold. They weren't used to being out on a night like this. The two dogs were normally fully laid out in front of the huge roaring fire and Colonel Gepsy sat in his large leather, studded high back chair with a glass of whisky in one hand and a book in the other, waiting for the cook to say that dinner was ready. He shuffled his feet impatiently.

'Well, Jebb, I'll give her a few more moments, then we'll head for home, what?'

Jebb grunted disapprovingly.

Mrs Fox caught the sound of voices on the wind. She stopped dead and listened intently. It was Jebb and the Colonel. She stared through the thickly falling snow and could just make out the figures of two men and four dogs by the Land Rover. The two Alsatians and Labradors suddenly pricked their ears and started to bark.

'She's about,' shouted Jebb.

Mrs Fox knew the game was up, she had to make a break for it. Down the hillside she bolted like a ball from a cannon.

'There she is.'

The Colonel instantly turned on the lights and shouted, 'Present arms, fire at will.'

The Colonel was now in his element, this reminded him of his rip-roaring army days. Mrs Fox was weaving, ducking and diving as continuous shot ripped into the snow-laden banks. The smell of sulphur from the spent cartridges filled the air for a moment before it was whipped away in the prevailing wind.

'Bally brave fox,' shouted the Colonel.

'Not for much longer,' yelled back Jebb, hastily ramming two more cartridges into his twelve bore.

Mrs Fox continued her perilous descent, her little legs couldn't take much more. The shot was whizzing all around her causing the snow to explode ever nearer, she could almost feel the searing pain of torn flesh which she had experienced some years before.

I'm not going to make this, she thought to herself, then her cunning took over. A shot rang out, the closest one yet; she dived head long into the snow, over and over she rolled, the snow sticking to her beautiful bronze coat. Now she resembled a giant snowball as she continued to roll to the bottom. She came to rest at the side of the track where she lay motionless, cocooned in the snow.

'Good shooting, Jebb,' shouted the jubilant Colonel.

'Thank you, Sir, I've waited a long time for that.'

'Right, let's get the dogs into the Land Rover and go and survey our quarry, she will look quite dramatic over my fireplace.'

This was music to Mrs Fox's ears. While Jebb and the Colonel loaded up the dogs she took her chance.

She violently shook her snow-laden coat and darted across the track amongst the blackthorn and ash copse. There she stood for a moment, looking back in the direction of the Land Rover.

'Catch me now,' she sniggered, as she disappeared into the darkness.

Chapter Four

Abandoned

It was still a few miles back to her den and normally she would have done the journey in a couple of hours, but now, as the weather was so atrocious, it would take a lot longer.

It was now half past eight, she was very tired and cold. She had had to go through some very deep snowdrifts, some of which had covered her completely, and she had found herself having to burrow out of them.

'Oh dear, what a silly lady I have been. If only we hadn't caught that chicken and made the farmer angry I would have been home by now, nice and warm and dry in my den.

'It's no good, I'm going to have to find somewhere where I can have a sit down and rest awhile.'

She had just found herself a nice little place out of the bitter wind when she saw some car lights in the distance. They were coming along the road in her direction. She lay completely flat and watched intently as she knew that lights meant humans and mostly all of the humans she had come across had wanted to do her harm. She would lay there until the lights had gone, but they seemed to be slowing down. She tried to lay even flatter, her heart beating very fast, fear bubbling up inside of her. She knew she couldn't make a run for it because of the deep snow, so she would just have to lie there and hope that they hadn't seen her. The lights came to a stop and she could see someone in the car opening the door and throwing out what seemed to be quite a large object. The person then closed the door, the car engine revved up and away it went. Mrs Fox lay very still until she was certain that the humans had gone. She got up cautiously and was curious to know what had been thrown out of the car.

She shook off the snow which had stuck to her lovely bronze coat, looked around once more, then made her way over to where the large object lay. When she was within a few yards of it, she stuck her nose into the air and sniffed. There was a strange scent which she couldn't quite make out, she took a few steps more towards it and sniffed again. She could now see that it was a hessian sack, the sort that farmers use. Mrs Fox was quite used to what farmers did as she had paid their farmyards little visits to catch the odd hen when she was feeding her cubs, and on special occasions, like today.

One end of the sack was tied up with string. She warily took another couple of steps towards it when she saw it move. Mrs Fox jumped back startled and watched from a safe distance. The sack then remained still for sometime so Mrs Fox made her way back over to it once more. This time she could hear squeaking noises coming from inside the sack. Her instinct told her that whatever there was in this sack, was certainly not going to hurt her.

She went right up to it and put her nose to the ground and said in a soft voice, 'Is there anyone in there?'

She heard a couple of little sobs and then another couple of squeaks. Mrs Fox knew that there was something not quite right. She picked up the sack in her strong jaws and took it back to the little shelter she had found earlier. She set it down gently on the snow and began to bite at the knotted string. All the time she was doing this, the sobs became louder and louder.

After sometime, she managed to get the string off and open up the sack. To her astonishment there were two black and white balls of fluff huddled up together, then two pairs of frightened eyes full of tears turned and looked at her.

'Oh, you poor dears, what on earth has happened to you?'

She now realised that the humans she had seen throwing this sack out of the car had intentionally abandoned these two darling collie puppies. She also knew that if she had not found them they would have surely died. Mrs Fox now had to gather all of her strength and get these two forlorn little creatures back to her den as quickly as possible.

'Now then, you two, you mustn't worry any more, I'm going to take you back to my den where you can have something nice and warm to drink and a good sleep by a nice warm fire.'

The two puppies looked at Mrs Fox and thought what a kind lady she was. Their sobs were now beginning to subside.

'Now you must hold on tight as I am going to have to carry you home in this sack and we've got a long way to go.' She gave them both a warm smile as she could see that they were both very frightened indeed.

The snow was coming down very thickly, the wind was blowing and howling through the trees, it seemed angry with everyone and everything in its path. The sky was pitch dark and it was certainly not a night to be out in, let alone with two very small young puppies.

Well, the sooner we start, the sooner we will be home, she thought to herself, picking up the sack in her strong jaws, turning into the biting East wind once more, her battle now was against winter most gruesome. The two puppies tumbled backwards and fell to the bottom, upside down. One puppy started to cry but his brother put his front paw around him and snuggled up close.

'Don't cry, little one, I'm sure it's going to be all right. Don't you think that this lady seems kind?' They had never seen a fox before.

'Oh yes,' replied his little brother between sobs, 'but what if she isn't?'

The elder of the two didn't want to think that far ahead so he just snuggled up even closer and said with as much confidence as he could muster, 'Oh, she will be, now try and get some sleep.'

His little brother closed his eyes. He looked at him tenderly. Even though he was only a few minutes older, he had always been that bit bigger and more confident. He had bossed his little brother around in a nice way and took control of situations right from the start. Their mother hadn't scolded him, as he had done it so lovingly, she realised that all he wanted to do was

protect his little brother. He knew that their mother was no longer around, he missed her very much. He was aware that he must now take complete charge. The responsibility frightened him a little but he was determined that nothing or no one would ever come between him and his little brother. He now felt utterly exhausted and couldn't keep his eyes open any longer and drifted off to sleep.

Mrs Fox found the going extremely tough, but the more she thought of those two puppies, the more determined she became. She tried not to think of the driving snow, the gale force wind which she was battling against, as she struggled on. Her jaws were now beginning to ache with the weight of the sack. She couldn't see anything in front of her with the snow falling so thickly but her sharp instinct was now telling her that she was not far away from her home. Only one more field to cross, one more wall to climb over then she would be inside her wood.

This spurred her on. She couldn't wait to get home, her jaws, her neck and back were aching terribly, she was wet through and her paws were freezing cold. She was pleased she had got some wood in for her fire before she had gone to her friend's house, now all she had to do was light it.

She could now see the wall. She jumped on top of it, dragged the sack up and over then dropped it on the other side. She jumped down beside it, gathering it back up in her aching jaws, she was just yards now away from her front door. She was worn out, the night's activities having left her near broken. She could have so easily just laid down in the cold snow and gone to sleep. She could carry the sack no longer. She lay it on the ground and dragged it. The puppies had woken up.

They were totally disorientated, not quite knowing where they were and now what was this strange bumping on the ground? This really frightened them. The bumping stopped and they heard a door being opened, then they felt they were on the move again, then the door closed. They had at last arrived at the home of Mrs Fox.

Chapter Five

The Short Stay

They tumbled around in the sack as Mrs Fox lugged them down the small passageway to her sitting room where the fire was waiting to be lit. Mrs Fox was so relieved to be home out of the bitter gale-force wind and snow. She was completely shattered after her excursions, and all she wanted to do was curl up and sleep but her day was not yet done. First she lit her lamp and hung it up safely, she then peered into the sack. The two balls of black and white fluff were huddled up together looking very frightened and bewildered. The youngest one started to cry.

'There, there, my dears, we are home now, come on out of this wet sack. I'll just light the fire, it won't take long before it's roaring away and you'll soon be as warm as toast, then I'll go and make you some nice warm milk to drink.'

The two bedraggled puppies slowly clambered out, their eyes blinking in the bright light. They looked around at the new surroundings but they were much too tired and cold to take that much in.

Soon the flames of the fire were dancing merrily away, giving out a lovely warm glow. The two young

puppies lay down on the old hearth rug in front of it, while Mrs Fox returned with a couple of towels.

'Let's give you both a good rub down and get your circulation going again.'

She picked them up in turn and laid them on her lap and she gently rubbed them dry. She then laid them back on the hearth rug, they looked up at her, she was a nice kind lady with beautiful big brown eyes.

'Right, I'll go and get your warm milk, it should be ready by now.'

Mrs Fox got up out of the chair and went to her little kitchen. She poured out two steaming cups of milk. There wasn't enough for her as she had to leave enough milk for their breakfast in the morning; she would have a cup of camomile tea later. She took the two cups back into the sitting room and gave them to the puppies.

'Now don't drink it too quickly or you'll get tummy ache.'

The two puppies reached for the milk eagerly, they were ravenous, they couldn't remember the last time that they had had any milk. Mrs Fox sat by the fire in her old armchair looking down at the two little puppies. Her heart went out to them, they were so like her own cubs. She would have loved to have kept them and brought them up as her own but she knew deep down that she couldn't as she didn't have the resources. Food was so scarce in winter. Mrs Fox often came home after a night's hunting with an empty stomach so sometimes she would have to venture out in daylight hours to catch a mere morsel but it was very dangerous, especially now with the snow she could be seen for miles, her brown pelt against the white landscape. She was always very grateful though to Sophie for leaving dog biscuits outside her den, but these weren't enough to keep herself and two puppies alive for the next few weeks. She didn't know when she would be able to get any more milk so she had to find someone else who would take good care of them.

The two puppies finished their milk and gave back the empty cups licking their lips, their eyes full of gratitude. They both cuddled up together and went off to sleep most contented. Mrs Fox went into her bedroom and brought out two blankets, one to go over the puppies and one for herself! She wouldn't be going to bed tonight, she had too much thinking to do, she must try and solve the problem of where she was going to find a good home for them. But it wasn't long before her big brown eyelids closed over her big brown eyes and she fell fast asleep.

Early the next morning Mrs Fox woke with a start, 'Oh dear, I must have dropped off.'

She looked down at the puppies who were still fast asleep and looked so peaceful, much different to how they had looked the night before. Their fur had dried into a fluffy black and white mass by the fire and they looked so relaxed.

When they wake up, I must explain to them why I cannot keep them. However, she had thought of a plan and if it worked she would still be able to see them most days; she was acquainted with a wonderful family who would be just perfect to adopt the puppies. She felt very pleased with herself, she got up out of her armchair, yawned and stretched. Her back and neck still ached from the rigours of the night before and sleeping in an awkward position in the chair hadn't helped. She went to her bathroom, washed her face and brushed her teeth, then made her way to her kitchen. She divided the last drop of milk between the two cups and then made herself a cup of camomile tea.

'I wonder what the weather's like this morning. If it's anything like last night I won't be able to put my plan into action.'

She walked along her passage and unlocked the front door. She opened it nervously, it was very quiet, she opened it wider and what a beautiful sight. Everywhere was white. She went outside and looked around, the storm had completely died out, there was now only peace and tranquillity in the forest. The silence was interrupted only by the lovely song of the blackbird. The snow was very crisp underfoot and was glistening in the early morning sun which was filtering through the trees. It was a most glorious, almost magical morning.

'Good morning,' shouted Mrs Fox to her neighbours, Mr and Mrs Brocklehurst, who lived under the tree opposite.

They were showing a passing deer the state of their front door. It had been severely storm damaged and was just hanging on by one hinge. They turned around, 'Oh good morning, Mrs Fox, my my, what a storm we had last night.'

Mrs Fox nodded in agreement. She did not want to stay and have a conversation, she didn't have the time, as there was too much to do. Today was perfect to put

her plan into action and so she must get on. She hurried back into her house.

The two little puppies had started to wake up. They yawned and stretched their little legs and paws and felt decidedly comfortable but like all babies they have to be fed little and often and so they were beginning to feel hungry again.

'Good morning, my little brother, did you sleep well?'

'Oh yes, thank you, did you?'

'Mm, yes I did,' replied the elder brother, having another good stretch.

'I like it here and I like that lady, I hope we don't have to leave here ever; if I wasn't missing Mummy so much, I should be quite happy.'

The elder brother looked at his little brother and gave him a reassuring smile.

'I'm sure it will be all right, the lady wouldn't have taken all that trouble to rescue us and bring us all the way here if she hadn't meant to look after us.'

Mrs Fox had heard them waking up and had gone into the kitchen and warmed up the last of the milk. As she was coming into the sitting room she could hear what they were saying. Tears filled her beautiful brown eyes. If only she could keep them. She put down the tray with the cups of milk on and got out her hanky and wiped her eyes.

'Oh dear, I do hope they will understand what I've got to do. Oh, I hope they won't hate me for it.'

She composed herself before picking up the tray and entering the room.

Chapter Six

The Plan

'Good morning, my dears, I thought I heard you waking up. I've warmed up this drop of milk, so drink it up while it's still warm then I want to have a little chat with you.'

She sat herself down in her armchair and watched while the two little puppies drank their milk. When they had both finished she picked them up and gave them a big cuddle on her knee. She started to tell them that as much as she wanted to keep them with her it was impossible as she did not have enough food for three mouths to carry them all through to the spring.

It was the middle of winter and food was scarce, but she did know of a place where they would be very happy and get all the food, love and attention that they deserved. It was only a stones throw away, so she could see them as often as they liked. The little puppies listened intently becoming extremely frightened and confused once more. Tears spilled on to Mrs Fox's lap and they weren't just from the puppies. This was the hardest thing she had ever had to do.

Mrs Fox waited until the sun was quite warm, as warm as it could get on this cold winters day, before attempting to take the puppies outside. She went up

her passageway and peered outside her front door just to make sure that all was well. She was satisfied that this now was the right time. She walked back down the passageway and went into her bedroom. It was a dainty little room, all spick and span just like her sitting room and kitchen. There was a bed in the middle neatly made with a brightly coloured quilt on top, a little bedside table on one side and a chest of drawers on the other out of which she pulled the bottom drawer. Inside there were little clothes for little cubs all folded in an orderly fashion. She picked out two jumpers which she had knitted. The memories came flooding back of her own litter of cubs who had been dispersed by the local hunt several years earlier and now all lived far away with their own families. She had tried to find them and tell them about Hawkes Clump where the hunt and gun are no longer allowed and that they would be safe, but as yet, had heard nothing. She sighed sadly and closed the drawer. She went back to the sitting room where the two puppies were playing by the fire.

'Come on you two, it's time to get ready and for you to see your new home, now put these jumpers on so as not to catch cold.'

She pulled out the sack from her cupboard. The puppies were very frightened at the prospect of having to get back into it, but Mrs Fox assured them that it was the easiest way for her to carry them and they would be only in it for a short while. She then started to explain what she was going to do and told the puppies what they had to do. Mrs Fox now started to sound so confident that the puppies' spirits began to rise. They bundled themselves into the sack and held on to each other as Mrs Fox picked it up and off they all went. Outside, Mr and Mrs Brocklehurst the Badgers, were busily mending their damaged front door. Mr Brocklehurst had the saw sawing off the broken hinge and Mrs Brocklehurst was holding the door steady for him. They both turned in the direction of Mrs Fox when they heard her front door open and close but before they could say anything she had swiftly trotted off carrying the sack in her mouth. The badgers looked at each other with a raised brow then quickly returned to their carpentry. They had to get their door on before nightfall which came early this time of year and it could start snowing again anytime.

Mrs Fox also passed Mr Ronald Rabbit and saw Freddie Pheasant but she couldn't stop to tell them what was going on either as she hadn't the time. Anyway, she would see them all later and then tell them all about it. She walked through the wood which was pretty hard going as the snow was very deep. She kept on talking to the puppies just to reassure them that everything was all right. She reached the edge of the wood, put the sack down gently and peered over the wall. All was quiet. She picked it back up again and jumped over the wall and made her way into the centre of the field right in front of the windows of Sophie's house. Mrs Fox was certain that the puppies would be seen from here.

She lay the sack down gently and whispered to the puppies, 'You can come out now.'

The two little puppies were rather apprehensive at the thought of leaving Mrs Fox who had been so kind to them and, after being so warm, having to go back out into the cold again.

'Come along, my little puppies, you won't have to stay out here long, I'll make sure of that.'

The two puppies climbed out, they breathed in sharply as they met the freezing air. The snow was very cold and wet on their tummies as they crawled out and sat on top of the sack.

'Now then, my dears, I want you to cuddle up together and keep as warm as you can until we can attract their attention.'

Mrs Fox looked over to Sophie's house. She knew how much Sophie and her parents loved animals and she was certain that they would look after these two endearing little creatures.

She looked back to the puppies, 'Now then, I want you two to make as much noise as you can, and remember, you haven't been abandoned, I'm only just behind the wall, I'll be watching all of the time, and if you don't manage to make enough noise, I'll start howling.'

She bent down and gave them both a great big hug, then walked back over to the wood, hopped over the wall and disappeared from view. The two little puppies felt very much alone now out in this big field and very vulnerable. Mrs Fox had put them in a spot for all to see. There wasn't any shelter to hide behind or any milk to drink and all of a sudden the two little brothers had forgotten that Mrs Fox was behind the wall watching them and they began to panic. They felt as if they had been abandoned once again.

They then began to think of the family that lived in the little cottage opposite. They didn't know them, they were complete strangers and what if Mrs Fox was wrong and the family didn't want them? Their futures began to look very bleak once again. They cuddled up together like Mrs Fox had told them to keep themselves warm and then began to cry. First it was just a whimper and then it became full blown howling. Tears were rolling down their faces and they clung on to each other, never wanting to let go.

'That's the way, little ones, keep it up,' said Mrs Fox smiling to herself.

Little did she know that the puppies weren't acting, this was for real.

'With the amount of noise they're making, someone is sure to come out and investigate soon.'

Mrs Fox knew that at least one member of the family was at home as she had seen Sam looking out of the window when she had crossed the field with the puppies. She always felt very safe when he was around.

Chapter Seven

Dan and Tex

Sophie and her parents were inside the house having some toast and hot chocolate. They had already had their breakfast early and had been outside to inspect the damage that the storm had inflicted on them the night before. Sophie had finished off her snowman with a little help from Mummy and Daddy and as they had all been so busy, they had all got rather peckish.

So, at half past eleven Sam had shouted over to Audrey and Sophie, 'Time for elevenses, isn't it?'

'Okay, hungry Mr Papa Bear, Sophie and I will go and make a start, don't be too long in coming in,' and off they both went into the warm kitchen.

Sam was finishing off securing part of their conifer hedge. He and Audrey had planted it five years previously, but as it was so cold and open where they lived it had taken a long time to establish itself and was taking a long time to grow. The roots weren't as strong as they should've been, so Sam was securing the conifer trees to wooden stakes to stop the wind from blowing them down. They had taken quite a battering the night before and if they had another storm like it again tonight they would certainly be uprooted and it would be such a shame for that to happen as it would take another seven to eight years for new young conifers to become established and form a dense hedge. He finished securing the last tree then took himself off into the kitchen where Sophie and her mother had made hot buttered toast and hot chocolate.

'That smells good enough to eat,' said Sam taking off his boots and coat.

He walked over to the sink to wash his hands then sat down with Sophie and Audrey and tucked in. When they had all finished, Sophie helped her mother clear away the crockery, her father was looking out of the window.

'Well, the sky is still nice and clear, we should be in for a nice day. We can make another snowman if you want, Sophie?'

'Oh, yes please, Daddy, I'll just go and get my coat and hat.'

Sophie ran to the cloakroom to retrieve them and put them on.

'That's funny,' said Sam scratching his head, his face looking rather puzzled.

'What is?' asked Audrey, walking over to him to see what he was looking at.

'I could have sworn I just saw that old fox come out of the wood carrying a large sack in her mouth.'

'You've had too much snow,' said Audrey laughing as she walked back over to the sink. 'You'll be saying next that you've just seen the snowman walk past the window.'

Sam went over to her and put his arms around her waist, 'Oh, Audrey, I do love you. You're the best wife

and best mother that Sophie and I could ever have.'
'Oh, Sam, I love you too.' Audrey turned round from
the sink, put her arms around his neck and gave him a
great big kiss.

Sophie came in and caught them. 'Can I have one
too?'

Sam and Audrey laughed, 'Of course you can,'
picking her up between them and giving her a big kiss
and a cuddle.

Suddenly Sophie looked around and struggled to
get down.

'Did you hear that?' she asked. 'It sounded like
something crying.'

Sophie quickly put on her wellingtons and ran to
the door and went outside. She looked all around the
garden but couldn't see anything. Then she heard it
again. Sam and Audrey were watching her from the
door and then they heard it too. Sam put his boots and
coat on and followed Sophie outside. She was by the
wall trying to climb over as she was too small to see
over it.

'It's coming from the field, Daddy,' she shouted.

Sam ran over and saw two bundles of fluff crying
on a sack. He picked up Sophie who was now halfway
over the wall and put her in the field, then climbed
over after her.

'Look, Daddy, look,' shouted Sophie pointing to
them. 'What is it?'

'Well, we'd better go and have a look.'

Sophie and Sam ran over to the bundles in the field
and saw the two little puppies who were whimpering,
huddled up together and looking very frightened.

'Oh, Daddy, look, two little puppy dogs. And look, they're wearing little jumpers. Where have they come from? Oh Daddy, just what I've always wanted. Can we keep them please, oh, please, Daddy?'

Sam bent down and picked one up and gave it to Sophie to carry, he then bent and picked the other one up.

'Come on Sophie, we'd better get them inside in the warm and give them some milk'.

He picked up the sack which the two puppies had been laying on, then looked over to the wood.

I did see that old fox carrying a sack then, Sam thought to himself, *What a clever old fox. We'll look after them, old girl, don't you worry about that.*

He didn't realise that the old fox was on the other side of the wall in the wood, watching everything that was going on. She knew that she'd done the right thing and that they would be well looked after. She watched them all go into the house, then turned and went home herself. She was so tired all she wanted to do now was sleep.

The two little puppies were very relieved to be found but still a little frightened. They didn't know if this family would want to keep them. They didn't know this family at all, not like Mrs Fox, but they need not have worried because when the little girl cuddled them both so carefully and they heard her sweet gentle voice, they knew that they would be very happy with them. They were taken back to the house and put in a basket with a lovely soft blanket, and placed by the Rayburn. They were then given some milk and soon they were both fast asleep, looking most contented and happy. They both knew then that they would be the most loveable, most loyal and obedient dogs in all of the world.

Sam and Audrey looked at Sophie who was sat by the basket, unable to leave the puppies alone, she loved them so much already. She was the happiest little girl in the world, and she, too, vowed that they would be the best looked after and most loved dogs in all of the world.

Sophie was too excited to sleep that night. Her mother heard her tossing and turning in bed so she went up to see her. Sophie talked non-stop about the puppies and what she was going to call them.

Little did she know that Mrs Fox had come into the garden and was under Sophie's bedroom window listening. She heard Sophie say she was going to call them Dan and Tex. She liked those names, they suited them so well.

She smiled to herself and went trotting off back through the wood. At home she discovered, lying before her front door, two little jumpers folded very neatly. She knew that Sam had put them there and she also knew that there were going to be some great adventures ahead for all of them.